MW00980293

THE ADVENTURES OF
SEEK & SAVE

THE
GREAT
ESCAPE

WRITTEN BY
SHARON SWANEPOEL

A GOD'S GLORY MEDIA PUBLICATION

Copyright ©2014 Sharon E. Swanepoel
All rights reserved under international copyright law. No part of this book may be reproduced or transmitted in any form or by any means, electronic or mechanical, including photocopying, recording, or by any information storage or retrieval system, without the written permission of the author.

Author: Sharon Swanepoel
sharon@godsglory.org

Illustrator: Lucas Loscinto
lucas.loscinto@facebook.com

Illustration Graphics,
Layout and design:
Rudi Swanepoel

The Adventures of Seek and Save:
The Great Escape
ISBN: 9780977264797

Dedicated to
Gene Howard Brown.
(1941 - 2013)
He, together with his wife, Chris, caught the vision of Seek & Save and ran with it, sharing in our adventures with God and leaving a lasting legacy for the Kingdom of God.
Forever in our hearts.

- Thanks to my Heavenly Father, Whom I love infinitely, with my every breathe may Your glorious love be shown as we declare Your Gospel and make Your presence known. Living for You always.
- Thanks to my husband, Rudi, your input and that of the Holy Spirit has shaped me and your belief in me is the thrust to do what I never imagined possible. Thank you for the hours of work on the graphics, layout and design of this project. I love you.
- A big thank you to our God's Glory partners and ministry friends, as well as our family for your prayers and support. We love you.
- Our God's Glory Board of Directors: Herb & Anita McDermott and Bill & Lynna Roberts, thank you for trusting in the vision God has given us and supporting us all the way. We love you.
- All who helped and participated in the Seek & Save Projects and fund raising efforts, especially Chris Brown, we love you and pray the Lord's richest blessing upon ya'll.
- Joyce Squires, thank you for helping with the editing. You are a blessing as always. We love you.
- Lucas Loscinto, thank you for the illustrations. You are in our prayers always. We love you.
- To all the churches who participate in the Seek & Save Projects. Our combined efforts: a lasting impact. We love you.

P. O. Box 1430, Dacula, GA 30019. / www.Godsglory.org
Printed in China

Hello boys and girls. Allow us to share this story
Of how TELL's life was changed from doom to glory.
Are you ready to hear how his life became ever new?
Listen well and we will tell you.

The SEEK and SAVE team of two became a team of three.
When TELL was added after he was set free.

SEEK and SAVE were thankful for a beautiful day
SAVE drank his coffee and SEEK sipped his tea
Before heading out, the city sights to see.
While wondering what adventure today would bring
SEEK thought of a song to sing.

H-A-P-P-Y... I'm so....
Happy, happy, happy, I'm as happy as can be.
Happy, While I drink my steaming cup of tea.
Happy, happy, happy, There's a whole wide world to see.
Happy, To know Jesus. Yes, He cares for me.

H-A-P-P-Y... I'm so....

Happy, happy, happy, Counting blessings one, two, three.
Happy, On my face, it's very plain to see.
Happy, happy, happy, Showing others, they can be.
Happy, As I'm sharing, the joy that's within me.
H-A-P-P-Y... I'm so.... HAPPY!

SEEK and SAVE were always rescuing people in trouble
Sorting out problems of those who were caught up in a muddle.
They loved to sing and wondered what adventure today would bring?
Sipping on their steamy brew they were deciding what to do...

It was a fatal blow
DESTROYER despised SEEK and SAVE so!
Almost crippled he winced away from the fight.
Fading away into the night.
He pondered and wondered:
Why SEEK and SAVE just had to show up,
His perfect destruction plan to disrupt!
There was no defense against their attack!
They were fearless and made him panic,
This was a major setback!
After all sin's destruction is making a comeback!
Losing to SEEK and SAVE was a huge drawback.

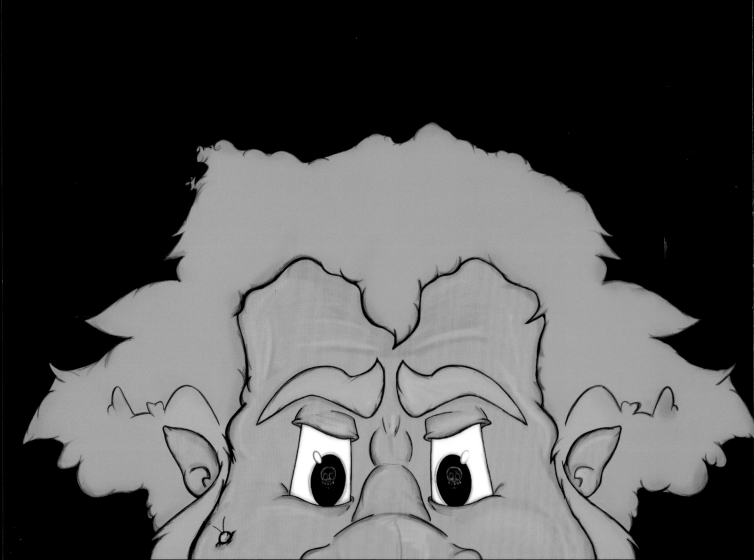

DESTROYER would set a snare and wait
To make sure that, whoever got stuck,
Death would be their fate.

He would devise their demise.
His snare in disguise,
Was the trap they would despise
And their bondage was his prize.

There was a beautiful rainbow in the sky
Sidewalks once wet were now dry.
The unsuspecting villagers did not see him there
He was hiding in the shadows away from the sun's glare,
He carried it with him, this destructive snare.
It would destroy somebody for sure and he didn't care.
He cunningly placed it where he knew it would be found
Somebody was coming, he flinched at the sound.
Soon they would find it and to sin they would be bound
Smiling he hid himself by sliding snakelike to the ground.

DESTROYER was a hideous creature
With not one good feature.
He was a deceiver and bad at the core
Destroying others would settle the score.
He used to be beautiful indeed
But his pride made him ugly and destruction was his creed.
He loved the night and hated day,
He hated truth and believed lying was the best game to play.
His skin was slimy, cold and wet,
Grey all over and his hair unkempt.
His teeth were crooked and sharp as knives
Death could be seen in his eyes.

He sneared with glee as he saw his victim approach
Yet another loser that he could load with reproach.

TELL loved the smell of the air after the rain,
So he decided to go for a walk.
There he met a man, named LAWMAN LEGAL,
And they started to talk.
"Perfect!" said DESTROYER to himself.
It was TELL. DESTROYER knew him well.
A lie teller, fibber, TELL would be
Teller of truth will never be his destiny.

TELL came closer and DESTROYER shivered with delight
TELL approached the snare inquisitive at the puzzling sight.

"I know what that is!" LAWMAN LEGAL said,
While nodding his head.
"That is called the snare of sin and try as you might
If you get into the snare, to sin you are fastened tight!
Don't go near it just walk away, hear what I say!"

TELL asked, "Why?"
For he thought LAWMAN LEGAL a wise guy!
LAWMAN LEGAL continued,
"Once you step in you will get stuck."
Nodding in agreement to himself he repeated,
"Stuck! Oh yes, Stuck!"
TELL said, "Oh LAWMAN LEGAL,
I don't believe in your warning,
I believe in luck."

Hiding in the shadows,
DESTROYER sent one of his friends, JACKPOT NILL by.
She whispered, "Get in TELL, you can do it, give it a try.
Roll the dice and spin the wheel
Win the jackpot your fate to seal.
Life's just a gamble; it is just one more dare.
You've got nothing to lose so what do you care.
It's like winning the lotto, take the gamble, LUCK is the motto."
Hearing what she said TELL wandered over and stepped into the snare.
"OOH, AAAH, MMMM" TELL enjoyed every moment,
He was unaware that his current action would lead him to despair!
He said, "I feel lucky and this feels great!"
Then he tried to move his feet and realized his mistake!
Could it be? Sure enough he was stuck!
He yelled, "Good riddance to luck!"
JACKPOT NILL giggled, "Life is just a game we play."
Then she cowardly ran away.
LAWMAN LEGAL said, "TELL, stuck in the snare you will ever be!
You should have listened to me!
It will take a miracle to set you free!"
And with that said,
LAWMAN LEGAL walked away while shaking his head.

DESTROYER squealed in delight at the sight.
"Ha! TELL, your luck got you stuck"
He whispered with glee
Thrilled as he listened to TELL's plea...
"Help me, please help me!" TELL cried out!
"I'm stuck, I'm stuck!" He let out a shout!

JACKPOT NILL

He tried to set himself free,
Then he saw somebody approaching and wondered, who could it be?

TELL was stuck in the snare. This is tragic!
DESTROYER sent ABRA CAZABRA to bring the magic.
This would ensure that TELL, in the snare was fastened tight.
For escape was impossible, try as he might.

ABRA CAZABRA walked by giving TELL the evil eye.
TELL asked, "Who could you be?"
"ABRA CAZABRA is my name, I am a witch, and magic is my fame,
You look puzzled to me, I have the solution, I hold the key."
TELL asked, "What can you do, please help me?"
"I will give you a fetish and curse, that's all you need.
Take this wand, drink that potion and magically you will be freed!
Witchcraft is my superpower
And you will be set free within the hour.
Here you go, just give it a try. I have to go now, so bye-bye."
Magic could be the answer! TELL could not delay.
He watched in awe as ABRA CAZABRA mysteriously walked away.
Then deep in thought he said, "Now let me see.
Here snare, take the curse and the fetish so I can be free!"
TELL waited and the hour past, still his bondage continued to last.
In a muddle to solve this puzzle
He was troubled and struggled.
He winced and wheezed.
"Help, me!" He pleaded.
TELL, now bound tighter than before, cried out, "Magic is a lie!"
"I've got to get free I just have to try!"
He tried everything to set himself free.
Then once more he saw somebody approaching, who could it be?

DESTROYER smiled in an evil grin,
He whispered, "I always win,
I own luck you see, It all belongs to me!
Now, little TELL, you are stuck and out of luck!"
Then, like a crazed chicken he chuckled,
"Cluck, cluck!"

Then DESTROYER sent DIZZY DAZE another faithful friend,
Saying, "I strongly recommend that you get TELL drunk and high!
For once he has started, I know TELL will give it another try."

DIZZY DAZE staggered by looking drunk and very high.
TELL asked, "Who could you be?"
He hiccuped, "HICCUP! Oh, excuse me.
DIZZY DAZE is my name,
Party is my game.
I crave to get high and just let life pass me by.
But dude, you have a problem I see.
I have the solution just ask me."
TELL asked, "So what can you do? Please, help me!"
"Drugs and alcohol is all you will need.
Smoke, snort, shoot and drink it, at great speed."
Here you go, just give this a try.
It's time for me to get high, I have to go now, so bye-bye!"
TELL followed his advice
Was DIZZY DAZE right? TELL felt as high as a kite.
TELL said, "Now let me see.
Here snare, take the drugs and alcohol so I can be free!"
With his head pounding and his vision impaired,
The more he used the tighter he was ensnared.
Feeling sick, he said, "This is not helping,
Drugs and alcohol is a lie!
I've got to get free, I just have to try!

BIGGY BUCK$

"It is now time for my secret weapon."
Announced DESTROYER, who was giddy with pleasure,
"BIGGY BUCK$ who brings envy, greed and lust for treasure!
Funny how money can brighten one's mood!
Those who have not, desire and it poisons their attitude.
Some crave money galore
And chase after it to make more and more,
Deceived that money is all they need.
Like a worthless weed, greed will succeed,
To rope them with its roots and never satisfy their need."

As TELL started to cry he saw BIGGY BUCK$ flashing by
With gold and silver in abundant supply.
TELL asked, "Who could you be?"
The stranger answered, "You have a problem I see.
My name is BIGGY BUCK$ and I have a solution deluxe."
TELL asked, "What can you do to help me?"
"Money sonny, money holds the key."
TELL said, "Oh, please I want some, in this' I can believe!
Money is what I want and all I really need.
You will be doing a good deed and I will be freed."
BIGGY BUCK$ was feeling generous indeed
He was not in the mood to hear TELL plead.
So he said, "Here, poor thing, just give it a try, my time is money.
I have to go now so bye-bye."
TELL said, "No, don't go home,
I don't want to be stuck here on my own!"
BIGGY BUCK$ and his money walked away
There was nothing more to say.
For, money passes quickly and money would not stay.
TELL looked down and thought, this could be the answer!
"I have no doubt. It will work, I can buy my way out!"
Now let me see... "Here snare, take the money so I can be free!"

He was troubled and struggled, he winced and wheezed.
"Help me, help me!" TELL pleaded.
"This is not helping, money is a lie!
I've got to get free, I just have to try!"
TELL, tried again to set himself free.
Once more he saw somebody approaching
And wondered who this would be?

DESTROYER had a brand new scheme,
"ON-A NIRVANA" he said to himself as his eyes started to gleam.
"It is time for confusion,
She's the one to convince TELL that being stuck is just an illusion,
My subtle deceiving will soon have TELL believing."

ON-A NIRVANA glided by.
TELL said, "Hello." ON-A NIRVANA did not reply.
He tapped her on the shoulder and asked, "Who could you be?"
"Oh sorry, ON-A NIRVANA is my name
Looks to me you have a problem getting free."
TELL asked, "Can you help me?"
"Let me look you in the eye MMm.
Yes, meditate, the solution is meditation and out you will fly.
Into a deeper consciousness you will go....
Here just do this HUMM MUMM OHH!
Hang this special crystal round your neck...
Clear your mind, relax, you're a total wreck!"
TELL tried and got it all wrong.
He imagined the snare was gone.
But as he looked down he frowned at the sight,
For there it still was and he was fastened tight.
ON-A NIRVANA said, "Stop your confusion
The snare's just an illusion."

"Give it a try,
I have to go now so bye-bye."
TELL let out a deep sigh!
"No, don't go home,"
TELL said, "I don't want to be alone."
"Sorry but I can't hang around,
Your bad aura is bringing me down!"

TELL looked down and thought, this could be the answer!
Now let me see... This has to work to set me free!
"Into a deeper consciousness now I go...
HUMM, MUMM, OHH!"
TELL looked down,
There it was, he was still in the snare tightly bound!

TELL saw something appear that was not there before,
Chains galore thick and bulky round his core,
They tightly bound him, it was sore!
As he struggled he was fastened all the more
"I've got him, he's mine!" DESTROYER applauded,
"My efforts to destroy TELL are well rewarded."

TELL was troubled and struggled, he winced and wheezed.
"Help me, help me!" Came his plea!
"This' is no illusion, meditation is a lie!
I've got to get free I just have to try!

Nothing is helping! I am still stuck in this sin!
Help me, help me!" TELL cried out,
"I'm stuck! I'm stuck!" He let out a shout!
The chains were squeezing round his chest
And his breathing was stressed at best.
"I'm doomed; I have tried everything to set myself free!"
TELL then started to cry bitterly...

SEEK and SAVE decided to take a walk
SAVE nodded his head as he listened to SEEK talk.
Ever on the lookout for people in need
SEEK and SAVE were at the ready,
DESTROYER'S plans to impede.
They would forever proceed
And ensure every victim freedom, guaranteed.
DESTROYER watched in terror as SEEK and SAVE walked by.
He tried to run interference
And made a lot of noise to drown out TELL'S cry.
SEEK'S senses were keen
And aware that DESTROYER was hiding behind the scene.
SEEK and SAVE knew all of DESTROYER'S schemes.
SEEK saw TELL first and said, "There is a man stuck in a snare,
He is crying, he must be in despair."
TELL gasped, as they walked closer and asked,
"What's the matter and how can we help?"
Sobbing, TELL said, "Help me get out.
Is there a solution you could tell me about?"

SAVE said,
"Tell us, how did you end up this way?"
"Well," said TELL, "I did not listen when LAWMAN LEGAL
warned me to just walk away!
I did not listen, if only I had obeyed!
I have tried so many things to set myself free.
I took a gamble that money, magic, witchcraft, new age,
drugs and alcohol was the answer for me.
I've tried them all. They could not set me free!
If there is a solution, what could it be?"

SEEK said, "JESUS is the Solution.
For the problem of sin is very big you have a great need.
However, if you repent of your sin you will be freed."
JESUS is the solution to your problem. He is all that you need.
Ask him into your life and you will be free indeed.
Stuck in sin you are doomed you see!
JESUS will help you, He will answer your plea.
His great love for you holds the key.
If you are ready to be set free, just say this prayer after me."

SEEK, SAVE and TELL prayed together
For JESUS is the only Way to get rid of sin's snare of terror.

Dear JESUS,
I ask you to come into my heart today
Come and wash all guilt and sin away
Forgive me for in sin I went astray
All this in JESUS' Name I pray
Amen.

The chains that bound him fell into the dirt,
He could breathe again and no longer hurt.
SAVE said, "TELL, now listen to me
"In JESUS' name you are set FREE!"

TELL said, "I can't believe this has happened! Can it be?
Once I was bound, now I am free!"
DESTROYER let out a groan then loudly screamed,
"I just hate it when they become redeemed!"

DESTROYER hissed, "TELL believe me,
You will fail again, just wait and see."
"No DESTROYER, you speak lies!" TELL said.
As DESTROYER's eyes red, now turned dead.
"JESUS came to seek and save me,
And with His love set me free."
TELL continued to say, "JESUS set me free, and I am oh so happy!"
"NO!" DESTROYER cried, looking scrappy.
"I can't hear this, be quiet, I insist!"
TELL replied, "In JESUS' name, DESTROYER, you I resist!"
Those words were like a punch to DESTROYER's gut.
DESTROYER had to retreat, tail between his legs like a beaten mutt.

TELL turned a corner in his life that day,
The very moment his sin was washed away.

Then TELL heard an alarming sound, voices crying, "We are bound!"
Carefully he tread, towards the sound on ahead,
What did he see? Could it be?
He looked on in disbelief, there were others snared in grief.
Four children stuck in the snare where he used to be...
Sin had got the best of their curiosity,
TELL just had to share how he had been set free.
He said, "ARNO, ZUAN, TY and CHARLIE, please now listen to me..."
So he told them his story of JESUS that brought liberty.

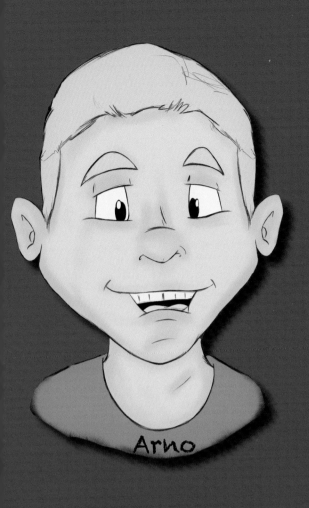

Arno

Zuan

Just in time, SEEK and SAVE walked by,
They too had been drawn by the children's cry.
SEEK, SAVE and TELL became a team that day,
To share the Good News that JESUS takes all sin away.
After prayer the children were without a tearful frown
And joyfully were jumping up and down.
There were big smiles on their faces,
Sins forgiven, they were in God's good graces.

With those big smiles their joy was on display.
They made their minds up that day,
Never again in the snare of sin to play!
All four promised to warn others to stay away.
Then thanked SEEK, SAVE and TELL and went on their way.
Oh what a happy day!

It was another fatal blow...
DESTROYER just despised SEEK, SAVE and TELL so!
He had to come up with a new scheme
Now that TELL was part of the SEEK and SAVE team,
Crippled, he winced away from the fight,
Fading away into the night.

Would you like to say the prayer like TELL?
If your answer is yes, you will do well.
Maybe you have got stuck in sin's snares
Let me tell you how much JESUS cares.
He has made a way for you to be free
In His love there is liberty.
For God so loved the world that He gave JESUS, His only Son
So that the destructive snare of sin can be overcome.

JESUS has come to SEEK and SAVE all who are lost
Nothing else can buy you out
JESUS paid the price that sin cost.

Satan, the destroyer, cunningly goes round
His delight to see people bound.
But the TRUTH, JESUS is to be found
Freedom from bondage no matter how tight you are bound.
Bondage and shackles disappear,
The Deliverer, JESUS, is near.

Only JESUS can save you for He paid the price
He has conquered Satan's every vice.
Don't settle for just a temporary fix
The lure of sin is part of the devil's box of tricks.
Seeing you stuck is how he gets his kicks.

Now say this prayer after me
And just like TELL you will be free!

Dear JESUS,
I ask you to come into my heart today
Please wash all my guilt and sin away
Forgive me that in sin I went astray
Teach me to walk in You, the Way.
As all my cares and burdens on you I lay
Thank you for loving me, come what may
Show me your will in all I do and say
All this in JESUS' Name I pray.
Amen.

MEMORY VERSES

Romans 5:8
But God demonstrates His own love toward us, in that while we were still sinners, Christ died for us.

1 John 1:9
If we confess our sins, He is faithful and just to forgive us our sins and to cleanse us from all unrighteousness.

Romans 6:23
For the wages of sin is death, but the gift of God is eternal life in Christ Jesus our Lord.

Galatians 5:1
Stand fast therefore in the liberty by which Christ has made us free, and do not be entangled again with a yoke of bondage.

Luke 19:10
For the Son of Man has come to seek and to save that which was lost."

John 3:16
For God so loved the world that He gave His only begotten Son, that whoever believes in Him should not perish but have everlasting life.

QUIZ TIME WITH TELL

1. Who set the trap for TELL?
2. Who said, "Witchcraft is my superpower"?
3. What did LAWMAN LEGAL say it would take to set TELL free?
4. Who said, "Life's just a gable, it is just one more dare"?
5. Did TELL listen to LAWMAN LEGAL's advice?
6. What did TELL first say he believed in?
7. Who is the only Way to get rid of sin's snare?
8. Who told TELL that money was the answer and he could buy his way out?
9. Who came to SEEK and SAVE the lost?
10. Who was hideous with not one good feature?
11. Who prayed together in JESUS Name to set TELL free?
12. A teller of truth was TELL's destiny, what did DESTROYER want TELL to be?
13. Who told DIZZY DAZE to get TELL drunk and high?
14. If you repent, Who will forgive you of your sin?
15. How did TELL chase DESTROYER away?
16. Who is on the lookout for people in need, DESTROYER to impede?

ANSWERS:

1. DESTROYER
2. ACRA CAZABRA
3. A Miracle
4. JACKPOT NILL
5. No
6. Luck
7. JESUS
8. BIGGY BUCK$

9. JESUS
10. DESTROYER
11. SEEK and SAVE
12. A fibber / Teller of lies
13. DESTROYER
14. JESUS
15. TELL resisted him in JESUS' name
16. SEEK and SAVE

ACTIVITY CORNER

HELP TELL AND HIS FRIENDS FIND JESUS

FINISH

UNSCRAMBLE THE WORDS

1. eynom - _____
2. gygib $ubck - _____
3. gacim - _____
4. raba zaacrab- _____
5. cluk - _____
6. jtokacp liln - _____
7. dimeniotat - _____
8. no-a arninav - _____

Answers:
1. Money
2. Biggy Buck$
3. Magic
4. Abra Cazabra
5. Luck
6. Jackpot Nill
7. Meditation
8. On-a Nirvana

WHICH IS DIFFERENT?
CAN YOU FIND THE PICTURE THAT IS DIFFERENT ?

Answer: 5

Answer:2

Answer:3

|||||||||||||||||||||||||||||||||||||||||||||||||||||||||||||||||||||||||||||||||||||||||||||||||||

WORD SEARCH
LOCATE THE WORDS IN THE PUZZLE

C A N Y U T I M O N E Y J D F R E E
T L A T S T Y G V I N B G O P I J H G
L O S E A T V S E E K P A R U F A T F
C V F A V E F T V R S A D E R F S I N
P E M R E N H U J E S U S D E S A W
R F R T D E S T R O Y G F T F T G I H

1. SEEK	4. LOVE	7. TEA	10. SAD
2. SAVE	5. DESTROY	8. SIN	11. LOSE
3. JESUS	6. MONEY	9. FREE	12. SAW

JOIN THE SEEK AND SAVE ADVENTURE

Now that you are free, tell others too.
Share the Gospel message of how JESUS made you new.

How wonderful to tell the greatest story ever told,
A message that will never grow old.
JESUS has come to seek and save the lost
And on the cross, He paid the ultimate cost.

If you don't tell them they might never know
This good news you must not only tell, but also show
Do not stop at one, let the whole world know
Read the Bible and in God you will grow.

SEEK and SAVE'S mission team
Makes DESTROYER, the devil, scream!

SEEK AND SAVE

ADVENTURE MAP

COUNTRIES THAT SEEK AND SAVE HAVE BEEN TO:

2009-	Tbilisi, Republic of Georgia
2011 -	Tbilisi and Rustavi, Rep. of Georgia,
2011 -	Yerevan and Vanadzor, Armenia
2011 -	Western Cape, South Africa
2011 -	Gold Fields, South Africa
2012 -	Free State, South Africa
2013 -	Morogoro, Tanzania
2013 -	Cleveland, Ohio, USA
2013 -	Eau Claire, Wisconsin, USA
2013 -	Crowley, Louisiana, USA
2013 -	Western Cape, South Africa
2014 -	Huntsville, Alabama, USA
2014 -	Kwazulu-Natal, South Africa
2014 -	Western Cape, South Africa

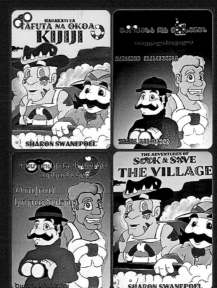

(A total of 100,009 Seek & Save Books printed and distributed)

For more information about the Seek and Save Books and Project visit:

www.SeekandSave.us

www.facebook.com/SeeknSave.org

PHOTO GALLERY
Children everywhere love the Seek & Save books!

Pictures taken in America, South Africa, Tanzania and Armenia.

MORE SEEK AND SAVE BOOKS

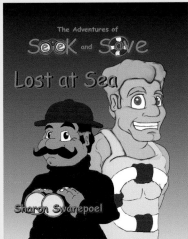
Lost at Sea

Lost in the Dark

The Village

For more information about the Seek & Save Books and Project visit www.SeekandSave.us

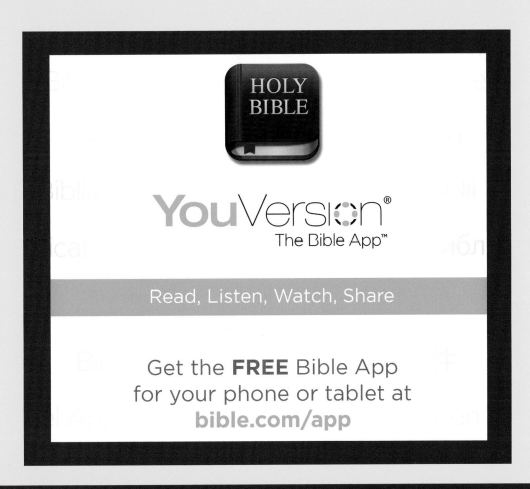

HOLY BIBLE

YouVersion®
The Bible App™

Read, Listen, Watch, Share

Get the **FREE** Bible App
for your phone or tablet at
bible.com/app

About the Author

Sharon Swanepoel

Sharon has a great love for children and a heart for evangelism. She travels the world with her husband, Rudi, sharing the Gospel of Jesus Christ.

She is a friend to the next generation. Projects like this one is driven by her passion to encourage children to know Jesus, while teaching them the core truths that will equip them for life. Her vision is to place books like this in the hands of children worldwide and thus share with them the Good News of Jesus Christ.

She is an accomplished musician / composer with several published CD's that can be downloaded from Itunes.com or CDBaby.com.

About the Illustrator

Lucas is an artist with a tremendous God-given ability to bring characters to life. He has a heart for children, and a passion for God.

Lucas Loscinto

About the Designer

Rudi joins his wife, Sharon, in reaching out to the next generation with a message of lasting hope and God's love. Being a communicator for many years, he understands the importance of getting your message across in ways to capture your audience's attention. Together Rudi & Sharon brought the many parts of this publication together into a potent, penetrating and passionate message.

Rudi Swanepoel